Sue Be...

Magic Ponies

A New Friend

Illustrated by Angela Swan

PUFFIN

To Silver – so exciting and an early inspiration

PUFFIN BOOKS

Published by the Penguin Group
Penguin Books Ltd, 80 Strand, London WC2R 0RL, England
Penguin Group (USA) Inc., 375 Hudson Street, New York, New York 10014, USA
Penguin Group (Canada), 90 Eglinton Avenue East, Suite 700, Toronto, Ontario, Canada M4P 2Y3
(a division of Pearson Penguin Canada Inc.)
Penguin Ireland, 25 St Stephen's Green, Dublin 2, Ireland (a division of Penguin Books Ltd)
Penguin Group (Australia), 250 Camberwell Road, Camberwell, Victoria 3124, Australia
(a division of Pearson Australia Group Pty Ltd)
Penguin Books India Pvt Ltd, 11 Community Centre, Panchsheel Park, New Delhi – 110 017, India
Penguin Group (NZ), 67 Apollo Drive, Rosedale, North Shore 0632, New Zealand
(a division of Pearson New Zealand Ltd)
Penguin Books (South Africa) (Pty) Ltd, 24 Sturdee Avenue, Rosebank,
Johannesburg 2196, South Africa

Penguin Books Ltd, Registered Offices: 80 Strand, London WC2R 0RL, England

puffinbooks.com

First published 2009
011

Text copyright © Sue Bentley, 2009
Illustrations copyright © Angela Swan, 2009
All rights reserved

The moral right of the author and illustrator has been asserted

Set in Bembo
Made and printed in England by Clays Ltd, St Ives plc

British Library Cataloguing in Publication Data
A CIP catalogue record for this book is available from the British Library

ISBN: 978-0-141-32593-4

www.greenpenguin.co.uk

RAINBOW MIST SCHOOL
CLASS GOLDEN FEATHER

My name is: Comet

My best friend is: My twin sister, Destiny

My favourite colour is: Purple

My favourite food is: Hay

I like to look after my sister

RAINBOW MIST SCHOOL
CLASS GOLDEN FEATHER

My name is: Destiny

My best friend is: My twin brother, Comet

My favourite colour is: All the colours of the rainbow

My favourite food is: Grass

I like to do dares and get into mischief!

Sue Bentley's books for children often include animals, fairies and wildlife. She lives in Northampton and enjoys reading, going to the cinema and watching the birds on the feeders outside her window. She loves horses, which she thinks are all completely magical. One of her favourite books is *Black Beauty*, which she must have read at least ten times. At school she was always getting told off for daydreaming, but she now knows that she was storing up ideas for when she became a writer. Sue has met and owned many animals, but the wild creatures in her life hold a special place in her heart.

Prologue

'Wait for me!' Comet cried, launching himself into the night sky.

Moonlight gleamed on the pony's golden wings, cream coat and flowing golden mane and tail. His deep violet eyes flashed as happiness flowed through him. He loved playing chase with his twin sister.

'Hurry up, lazy bones! You'll never catch me!' called Destiny. She swooped teasingly close and then shot upwards to hide in a fluffy cloud.

Comet noticed the rainbow dazzle of a jewel on a chain round her neck. He gasped. Destiny was wearing the Stone of Power! The stone protected the Lightning Herd they belonged to and kept them all hidden from the dark horses who would like to steal their magic. It was forbidden to take it from Rainbow Mist Island where they lived.

'Destiny! Wait! Come back!' Comet ordered.

But his twin's laughter floated towards him on the still, cold air. Comet flexed his golden wings and zoomed upwards in a spurt of speed. Soaring higher and higher, he burst through the cloud and emerged into star-studded blackness.

Destiny was just ahead of him. She turned and her ears twitched with mischief as she folded her wings and prepared to dive.

Comet called to her. 'No, don't! The Stone . . .'

Ching! There was a tiny sound in the silence as the chain round Destiny's neck snapped.

'Oh no!' A chill ran through Comet as the magic stone plunged into the lake below with barely a ripple.

Destiny's eyes widened in panic. 'What have I done?' she gasped.

'We must find the stone. Follow me!' Comet urged, flying down to the water and plunging in. Destiny followed him.

It was freezing cold and pitch black in the depths of the lake. The two ponies searched for a long time, but the stone was nowhere to be seen. Comet was ready to give up, when he saw a faint glimmer on the lake bottom. With one final effort, he dived and managed to pick up the stone.

'I have it!' But Comet broke the surface to find himself alone. Where was Destiny?

The young pony quickly flew home to Rainbow Mist Island to find his mischievous twin and tell her that all was well.

As Comet landed on the island's lush grass, an older horse with a wise expression stepped out from some trees.

'Blaze!' Comet dipped his head in a bow, before dropping the magic stone at the leader of the Lightning Herd's feet. It lay there glowing with shifting rainbow light.

'Well done, Comet,' Blaze said in a
deep voice. 'Your sister acted rashly, but
you have saved our herd from disaster.'

Comet defended his twin. 'Destiny
meant no harm. I'm sure she means to say
sorry straight away. Where is she?'

'Destiny has run away,' Blaze said gravely.
'It seems she thought the stone was lost
forever and was afraid that she would be
in terrible trouble.'

'But where can she have gone?' Comet
asked, puzzled.

'We do not know. You must ask for the
stone's help to find her.'

As Comet looked down at the stone,
it began to grow larger. Rays of dazzling
rainbow light spread outwards and an
image formed in the centre of it. Comet
saw Destiny's hooves touch down in an

unfamiliar forest in a world far away.

The magic pony felt a pang as he thought of his twin sister: lost, alone and in danger. He had to find her! There was a bright flash of dazzling violet light and a whirlwind of rainbow mist swirled round Comet. Where the magnificent winged-pony had been now stood a sturdy chestnut pony with a sandy mane and tail and glowing violet eyes.

'Go now, young friend,' Blaze urged. 'Use this disguise to find Destiny before she is discovered by the dark horses.'

Comet's chestnut coat bloomed with violet sparks. He snorted softly as he felt his magical power building. The cloud of rainbow mist began to spin faster and faster, and drew Comet in . . .

Chapter
ONE

'It's so gorgeous here!' Eleanor Gale
exclaimed. 'I can't wait to meet Aunt
Pippa's new ponies!'

She looked at Oak Cottage, which
stood on the edge of a forest. Roses
rambled round the front door and
colourful flowers filled the front garden.

Eleanor's mum smiled. 'Somehow
I don't think you're going to mind

spending the school holidays here while your dad and I are away.'

Both Eleanor's parents were musicians in an orchestra. She'd had the chance of going on tour with them, but had instead chosen to accept the invitation to stay with her aunt.

'Spending all day riding or hanging about in boring hotel rooms? It's no contest!' Eleanor said.

Her dad smiled indulgently as he began unloading her luggage. He wasn't at all horsey and was amused by Eleanor's obsession with ponies. 'Here you go.' He tossed her the bag containing her riding kit.

'Thanks!' Eleanor caught it deftly and walked through the front gate just as the cottage door opened and her aunt came out.

'Eleanor! It's great to see you!' Pippa Treacy gave her niece a hug. She was a tall slim woman with curly brown hair. Her eyes looked very blue in her tanned face.

'Hi, Aunt Pippa!' Eleanor returned the hug. 'I love your new cottage!'

'Me too. I can't believe that I've been here for six months already. You're my first staying guest.' Pippa was Eleanor's mum's older sister. She was a photographer and made her living from taking pictures of wildlife.

'How's the work going for your exhibition?' Mrs Gale asked.

'Don't ask!' Pippa sighed, tucking a strand of hair behind one ear. 'I've got so much to do. I can't believe I'm ever going to be ready.'

'Well – maybe Eleanor will be able to give you a hand with something,' Mrs Gale suggested. 'She's pretty good with a computer.'

'Um ... yeah,' Eleanor said, distracted. All she could think about was being allowed to ride her aunt's ponies soon. She was desperately going to miss her favourite pony, Patch, who she rode at riding school at the weekends, but being able to ride here every day definitely made up for it! She wondered if she would have a favourite at the end of the holiday – it would be like having her very own pony!

'I'm really sorry that we haven't time to come inside, but we're already running late,' her mum said, hugging her sister. 'I promise that we'll stay with you for the whole day when we come to pick up Eleanor.'

'See that you do!' Pippa said, smiling and wagging a finger. 'Well – you'd better get a move on or you'll miss your plane. Have a good trip. And don't worry about Eleanor. We'll be fine, won't we, love?'

Eleanor nodded at her aunt, kissed her mum and dad goodbye and then stood

beside Pippa to wave to them as they
drove off. She suddenly felt really sad at
the thought of not seeing them for six
weeks.

As soon as her parents' car was out of
sight, Aunt Pippa took Eleanor into the
cottage and showed her to her bedroom.
It was a pretty, sunny room at the back of
the cottage. From the window was a view

of the neat back garden, which had a gate
that opened directly on to the forest.

Eleanor noticed that there didn't seem
to be a paddock or any outbuildings.
She wondered where her aunt kept her
ponies.

Wow! This place is pony paradise, she
thought, looking at the pathways that
wound through the enormous trees
and the clearings of purple heather and
scrubby grass. Sun shone through the
trees and glinted on a little stream off to
one side. She imagined all the wonderful
rides she'd have.

'Can we go and see your ponies now?'
Eleanor burst out, unable to control her
excitement any longer. 'Are they at a farm
or a stables? How many have you got?
What are their names?'

Her aunt laughed. 'Slow down, Eleanor! One question at a time! I've got three: Mary, Jed and Blue. But going to see them is easier said than done. Free-ranging ponies can wander for long distances. It can take ages to track them down.'

Eleanor frowned. What did her aunt mean about her ponies being free-ranging? 'But I thought you owned them?'

'I do, but it's not quite that straightforward,' Pippa explained. 'I'm what's called a commoner. That's someone who lives in a house in the forest and who has certain rights – like the right to graze ponies in the forest. My ponies are wild and pretty much take care of themselves in the summer. They have a job to do, looking after the forest.'

Eleanor was fascinated. She had never heard of a commoner before. 'Are there lots of wild ponies living in the forest and looking after it?'

'About four thousand. They're all owned by other commoners. We take them hay in the winter, pay for health checks and make sure they wear fluorescent collars to keep them safe at night and so on. There are regular round-ups too, when the herds are thinned out and some of the ponies are sold.'

'But how do you find them when you want to ride them?' Eleanor asked eagerly.

Aunt Pippa looked surprised. 'I *don't* ride them. None of my ponies are broken in. I'm thinking of buying one to ride eventually, but it's just another thing I

haven't got round to.'

'Oh, right.' Eleanor didn't know what
to say. She wouldn't be able to do any
riding this holiday at all! Eleanor began
to miss her mum and dad even more and
wondered whether she should have gone
with them on tour after all.

She tried hard not to let her aunt see
how disappointed she felt. 'Well, I guess it

could be fun going out on a pony-hunt
to find Mary, Jed and Blue,' Eleanor said
with forced brightness.

'They are really quite special,' Aunt
Pippa said, smiling. 'That's why I love to
photograph them. I go out looking for
the ponies whenever I get the chance.
Even if I can't find them there are usually
others around.'

Eleanor cheered up a bit at the
prospect of meeting her first ever wild
pony. 'I'll just go and change my shoes
before we go into the forest! I'll be right
back!' she said eagerly.

Pippa laughed. 'Whoa there, young
lady! I didn't mean we could go right
this minute. I'm afraid I have to pop into
town now to collect some prints I've had
framed and to organize the invitations.

We can go out searching for ponies tomorrow or the day after. Why don't you come along with me for the ride? You could explore the local shops while I'm at the framers.'

Eleanor didn't really feel like shopping. 'I think I'll stay here and unpack, if that's OK.'

'Fine by me. But are you sure that you'll be all right by yourself?'

'Positive. I'm nearly ten now, Aunt Pippa. I'll sit and read in the garden when I'm finished.'

Pippa beamed at her. 'Goodness me! How grown up you are. Right then, I won't be long. I'll bring us something nice back for supper. How about pizza?'

Eleanor nodded. 'Sounds good.'

Her aunt went downstairs. Eleanor

heard a car start up and drive off. She
sank glumly on to the pretty patchwork
quilt that covered her bed and allowed
the disappointment to wash over her.

With no ponies to ride it looked like
this was going to be a very lonely holiday.
Aunt Pippa was lovely, but it was obvious
she was going to be really busy getting
ready for her exhibition over the next
few days. Eleanor tried hard not to wish
that she hadn't come. There wasn't even
anyone of her own age to hang around
with.

She got up and stowed her riding boots
and hat in the wardrobe as it didn't look
as if she'd have much use for them. After
piling the rest of her clothes into the
chest of drawers, she picked up her book
and went back downstairs.

Eleanor wandered slowly outside into the garden. She went and sat on the lawn for a while, enjoying the warm smell of newly cut grass. Mid-afternoon sun tipped the tops of the trees with dusty-gold light. A robin hopped on to a fence post, looking at Eleanor with its head on one side. It flew off as she put down her book, got up and walked to the bottom of the garden.

Resting her arms on the low garden gate, Eleanor stood staring across the forest clearing. Beyond the patches of heather and dusty-looking grass, she could see a rough path leading into a grove of birch, ash and oak. She wondered if her aunt's ponies might be somewhere in those trees, watching her with shy, wary eyes.

Suddenly, a sparkling rainbow mist filled the entire clearing, and Eleanor saw rainbow droplets forming and twinkling on her skin.

'Oh!' Eleanor screwed up her eyes to try to see through the strange mist.

As it slowly cleared Eleanor noticed that a pony had stepped out of the forest and was walking slowly towards her. It had a glossy chestnut coat, a sandy mane and tail, and large deep violet eyes.

'Can you help me, please?' it asked in a velvety whinny.

Chapter
TWO

Eleanor's jaw dropped as she stared at the
pony in utter amazement. She hadn't ever
seen a real wild pony before but she was
certain that they couldn't talk. She shook
her head. She must be imagining things.

She clicked her teeth encouragingly.
'Hello there. Aren't you gorgeous? I bet
you've come to see if Aunt Pippa's got
an apple for you. I wonder which one

you are: Mary, Jed or Blue?'

The pony's ears flickered and it lifted
its head proudly. 'I am neither of those.
I am Comet of the Lightning Horses. I
have just arrived here from Rainbow Mist
Island.'

'Y-you really c–can talk?' Eleanor
stuttered. 'How come?'

'All the magical Lightning Horses in my herd can talk. What is your name?' Comet asked.

'I-I'm Eleanor. Eleanor Gale,' she found herself saying. 'I'm staying here with my aunt for the summer holidays.' She felt like pinching herself to make sure she wasn't dreaming. But Comet still stood there, looking at her calmly. She noted with surprise that he had large bright violet eyes.

Comet dipped his head in a formal bow and his sandy mane swung forward. 'I am honoured to meet you, Eleanor.'

'Um . . . me too.' Eleanor still couldn't quite believe that this was happening, but her curiosity was starting to take over from her shock. Despite being wild, this magical pony didn't seem to be at all nervous of her. 'But why are you here in the forest?' she asked.

'I am looking for my twin sister, who is lost and in hiding,' Comet told her. 'She is called Destiny.'

'That's a lovely name. But who is she hiding from?' Eleanor asked, puzzled.

Comet's large eyes glistened with sadness. 'We were playing our favourite game of cloud-racing in the night sky when Destiny accidentally lost the Lightning Herd's Stone of Power. I found the stone, but Destiny thought it had gone forever and imagined she was in terrible trouble, so she ran away. The stone showed me that she is here, in your world. I must find her before she is discovered by the powerful dark horses who want to steal our magic.'

Eleanor frowned as she tried to take this in. It all sounded so strange and unreal – like a fairy tale. 'You say you and Destiny were *cloud-racing*? But how ...'

'Please, stand back,' Comet ordered, backing away.

Eleanor felt a strange warm prickling sensation flow to the tips of her fingers as violet-coloured sparkles blossomed in Comet's chestnut coat and a light rainbow mist swirled round him. The sturdy forest pony disappeared and in its place stood a handsome cream-coloured pony, with a flowing golden mane and tail. Springing from his shoulders were magnificent golden wings, covered with gleaming feathers.

Eleanor was speechless with wonder. She had never seen anything so beautiful

in her whole life.

'Comet?' she gulped when she could
finally speak.

'Yes, it is still me, Eleanor. Do not be
afraid.' Comet gave a deep musical neigh.
There was a final swirl of sparkling mist
and Comet reappeared as the sturdy
chestnut pony.

'Wow! That's a brilliant disguise! No one would ever know that you're not an ordinary forest pony,' Eleanor said.

'Destiny too will be in disguise. But that will not save her if the dark horses discover her,' Comet said gravely. 'Now I must look for her. Will you help me?'

Eleanor felt a second of doubt at the thought of the dangerous dark horses who were pursuing Comet's twin sister. But then the magic pony leaned forward and pushed his satiny nose into her hand.

Eleanor's soft heart melted as Comet huffed warm breath on to her fingers. 'Of course I will!' she said. 'We'll search for Destiny together.'

'Thank you, Eleanor.'

'I can't wait to tell Aunt Pippa about you! She'll be so –'

Comet lifted his head. 'No! You must tell no one about me or what I have told you!'

Eleanor felt disappointed that she couldn't confide in her aunt. She felt sure that Aunt Pippa could be trusted.

'You must promise,' Comet insisted, blinking at her with his intelligent deep violet eyes.

Eleanor nodded slowly. If it would help to keep Destiny safe until Comet could find her and return to Rainbow Mist Island, she was prepared to agree. 'OK. I promise. Cross my heart.'

'Thank you, Eleanor.'

'But where shall we start looking?' she asked. 'There are thousands of ponies in the forest. If Destiny's hiding among them it'll be almost impossible to find her.'

As Comet looked thoughtful there was
the sound of a car pulling on to the front
drive.

Eleanor started. 'Aunt Pippa! She's
back. I can't come with you now. She'll
notice I'm gone. I'll have to try to sneak
out later. You'd better hide before she sees
you!'

'Very well.' With a swish of his sandy

tail the chestnut pony turned and
galloped into the trees.

'Eleanor? Where are you, love? I hope
you like pepperoni on your pizza!' Aunt
Pippa called from the kitchen.

'I love it! Just coming!' Eleanor
answered.

As she went back inside, she bit back
a broad grin. It looked like her rather
lonely holiday had just taken a turn for
the better. Never in her wildest dreams
had she expected to make friends with a
magic pony!

Chapter
THREE

Eleanor's heart beat fast as she peeped into the sitting room, where Aunt Pippa was lying on the sofa, having a short rest after supper. All was silent, and then she heard a faint snore.

Smiling to herself, Eleanor tiptoed into the kitchen. She was already wearing her jeans and a long-sleeved top, and she sat on the back doorstep to pull on her

riding boots and hat. She felt tense with
excitement. Would Comet still be there?
Or would he have galloped off alone to
look for Destiny?

As Eleanor walked through the gate
at the bottom of the back garden, the
chestnut pony stepped out of the trees,
and a warm orange sunset glowed behind
him.

'You're still here! I'm so glad,' Eleanor
exclaimed.

Comet bent his neck to bump his nose
very gently against her arm. 'Greetings,
Eleanor. Climb on to my back. We must
go.'

Eleanor scrambled on to the chestnut
pony. She wasn't used to riding bareback,
but the moment she sat astride Comet
she felt perfectly at ease. His magic

seemed to spread over her, making her feel warm and safe.

She twined her hands in Comet's thick sandy mane as he leapt forward and galloped into the forest. Huge oak trees spread their branches overhead as they followed bridleways and paths. They came to a picnic area with a closed cafe and sped past, pushing deeper into the forest.

There was no one about. Most visitors had left to go home by now.

Eleanor and Comet weaved along twisting paths and tracks. In the warm glow of the setting sun they came upon small herds of ponies, grouped together in clearings or standing under the trees. Each time, Comet paused and trotted up to them, snorting a greeting, but they did not find Destiny among any of the ponies.

Comet galloped on tirelessly, his hooves skimming the ground. Eleanor crouched low on his back, feeling the breeze rush by, her hair streaming behind her. She was breathless with the thrill of riding the magic pony.

'Hold tight!' Comet told her as he surged up a hill topped by birch trees.

He paused at the top where the
ground fell away into a deep ravine and
a waterfall foamed into a river far below.
From their position on the high ground,
Eleanor could see the forest spreading out
in all directions – its hundreds of acres of
trees, divided by paths, clearings and roads
used by tourists and visitors.

'The forest is never-ending,' Eleanor
said. 'However will we find Destiny?'

Comet had stretched his neck and
was peering around with his keen eyes.
'Because we are twins we have always had
a special bond. If Destiny is close, I will
sense her presence. Also, if she has passed
by at any time she will have left a trail.'

'A trail? What will it look like?' Eleanor
asked.

'There will be softly glowing hoof-
prints, which are invisible to most people
in this world.'

'Will I be able to see them?' Eleanor
asked.

'Yes. If you are riding me or if I am
very close to you,' Comet told her. 'Are
you ready, Eleanor? We must keep
searching.'

'I'm ready!'

Comet sprang forward. He was

wonderful to ride – so smooth, fast and
exciting. Eleanor kept a close lookout
but she saw no sign of any magical hoof-
prints, and although they met other wild
ponies, none of them was Destiny.

Despite the thrill of riding Comet,
Eleanor felt her eyes drooping and she bit
back a yawn. The sun was now very low
in the sky and Eleanor knew that Aunt
Pippa might wake at any moment.

'You are tired, Eleanor,' Comet said
with concern. 'I will take you back now.'

Back in the clearing outside her aunt's
garden gate, Comet stopped and let
Eleanor slide from his back.

The pony's chestnut head drooped a
little. Eleanor guessed that Comet was
missing his twin sister.

'We'll find Destiny,' she said, gazing into his large sad eyes, which were as beautiful as amethysts. 'I promise I'll do all I can to help.'

'Thank you, Eleanor,' Comet said gratefully. 'I will see you very soon.' With a flick of his tail, he whirled round and melted into the trees.

Eleanor crept into the house and went swiftly upstairs. As she was taking off her riding boots and hat, she heard her aunt stirring. She stood at the top of the stairs just as Pippa came out into the hall.

'Goodness me! I must have dozed off. I think I'm ready for bed,' Pippa said, hiding a yawn behind her hand.

'Me too. Goodnight, Aunt Pippa. See you in the morning!' she called.

Tired, but with her thoughts still full of the thrilling forest ride, she went to her room, undressed and crawled into bed. Moments later, she was fast asleep.

Eleanor woke to find bright yellow light flooding into her room. She threw back the patchwork quilt, her mind buzzing with all that had happened yesterday. She

looked out of her window towards the
forest, wondering where Comet was and
what he was doing. She could see no sign
of him and she daren't call out in case
her aunt heard. Dressing quickly, Eleanor
hurried downstairs.

Aunt Pippa was in the kitchen making
breakfast. 'Good morning, love. Sleep
well?' she asked.

'Yes, fine, thanks,' Eleanor said, helping
herself to toast and scrambled eggs. All
she could think of was going into the
forest to find Comet, but she needed to
think of a reason for going off by herself.
Aunt Pippa wasn't just going to let her
wander off without knowing exactly
where she was going.

Eleanor puzzled over the problem as
she nibbled a corner of toast. She was

starting to think that it was all a bit
hopeless, and that it might even be the
last time she saw Comet, when the
telephone in the hall rang.

Aunt Pippa went to answer it and
returned looking a little flustered.

'That was the gallery. They're short-
staffed because of sickness and wondered
if I'd mind going in and hanging my

photographs,' she explained. 'I think I'm going to have to go over there. I'm sorry, Eleanor. It's going to be boring for you to come with me and sit around waiting.'

'Why don't I stay here? Then you won't have to worry about me,' Eleanor said helpfully, trying not to sound too eager. 'I want to finish my book anyway.'

Aunt Pippa looked relieved. 'Well, all right then. I hope I'll only be a couple of hours. Maybe we could go out and look for Mary, Jed and Blue after lunch?'

Eleanor nodded, smiling. 'I'd like that.'

As soon as she'd said goodbye to her aunt, Eleanor hurried upstairs to grab her riding boots and hat and ran out of the back garden gate. She stood in the clearing, her pulse quickening with excitement as she faced the trees and called Comet's name.

For a moment nothing happened
and she almost wondered if yesterday's
thrilling ride had been a dream. But
then the chestnut pony appeared out of
nowhere and walked towards her. His
sandy mane and tail stirred in the breeze.

'Greetings, Eleanor.'

'Comet!' Eleanor's heart lifted as she
looked at him, thinking how amazing

it was that he had chosen her to be his friend. Comet was her own special secret that she would never, ever tell anyone. 'I've got two hours to myself. We can go looking for Destiny again!' she cried.

Comet pawed at the ground, his deep violet eyes flashing with eagerness. 'Thank you, Eleanor. Climb on to my back.'

Chapter
FOUR

Comet set off in a different direction
from the one they had taken yesterday. As
they galloped between the trees, Eleanor
leaned forward and entwined her hands
in the pony's thick mane again. Comet
moved so smoothly that she felt like a
part of him and hardly even needed to
grip his sides with her legs.

It suddenly occurred to Eleanor that

she shouldn't ride Comet bareback and
without a head collar in broad daylight.
They hadn't met any other riders yet,
but when they did she was sure to attract
attention.

Comet's ears twitched back as if he
felt her hesitation and he came to a halt
beneath a large oak tree. 'Is something
wrong, Eleanor?'

'It's just that in this world ponies
usually wear saddles and bridles when
they're being ridden,' she told him.

Comet listened carefully as she
described the equipment in detail. When
she had finished, he nodded. 'I did not
know this. No one has ever ridden me
before. I will see to it now.'

Eleanor climbed down from Comet
and stood watching him curiously.

She felt a strange warm tingling
sensation in her fingertips as bright
violet sparks ignited in Comet's chestnut
coat. His ears and tail crackled with tiny
lightning bolts of magical power.

Eleanor's eyes widened. Something
very strange seemed about to happen.

She watched in complete astonishment
as with a whooshing noise thousands of
tiny glittery lights like busy worker bees
sprang into the air. The sparkling crowd
weaved back and forth. *Crackle! Rustle!
Clink!* The lights created a full set of tack
just as she'd described it.

'Wow!' Eleanor said breathlessly as
seconds later Comet stood there fully
tacked up.

'Is this right, Eleanor?' Comet asked, as
the sparks faded from his chestnut coat.

'It's just perfect!' Eleanor adjusted the
girth and slipped two fingers under the
strap to make sure it was firm but not
too tight round Comet's middle. She
mounted, checked her stirrup length,
picked up the reins and they set off again.

Eleanor and Comet rode along narrow
pathways, bordered by birch trees.
Gradually the trees grew more

thickly and shadowed the forest floor.
They rounded some bushes and came to
a clearing where a herd of about ten wild
ponies were gathered.

'Oh look. There are some young ones
with them. Aren't they gorgeous?' Eleanor
sighed.

Comet slowed to a walking pace.
He gave a friendly nicker as he moved
towards the rather nervous-looking
ponies. They turned their heads to look at

him, their ears twitching with curiosity.

Suddenly a dog came out of nowhere and shot straight past them. Barking loudly, it ran towards the herd. One of the young wild ponies reared up, its eyes rolling in terror.

'Bad dog! Get away from them!' Eleanor shouted. She twisted round to see if an owner was visible, but there was no one in sight.

The wild ponies stamped around, blowing in alarm. The youngsters seemed ready to bolt in all directions at any moment. Eleanor was worried that they'd injure themselves if they ran off in a blind panic.

'We'd better scare that dog off before those ponies scatter!' she cried.

Eleanor was about to squeeze Comet

gently and urge him forward, when he
tossed his head nervously and backed up.
She realized that he was also scared of the
dog. Perhaps they didn't have them on
Rainbow Mist Island.

'It's OK, Comet. I'll deal with this,' she
said, quickly dismounting and running
towards the dog. But now she was closer
to it, it seemed a lot bigger and fiercer.

'Go away! Go on!' she cried, waving
her arms.

The dog turned and looked at her and
a growl rumbled in its throat. It started
to walk towards her. Eleanor gulped and
began to back up slowly, regretting her
rash decision to face the dog alone.

She felt another prickling sensation
in her fingertips. It was a lot softer than
last time.

She glanced at Comet and watched as
the chestnut pony opened his mouth and
huffed out a big breath, which turned
into a miniature violet fireball. It shot
towards the dog, trailing bright sparks,
and hit it harmlessly on the nose before
dissolving into a puff of smoke. *Phut!*

'Yipe!' The dog gave a surprised yelp and dashed headlong for the trees with its tail between its legs.

Eleanor let out a sigh of relief. She walked back to Comet and patted his silky neck. 'Well done. That showed him! I was scared for a minute there.'

'It was very brave of you to try to scare that creature away. Thank you, Eleanor.'

'I didn't really think about it. I knew you were scared and I wanted to help. I'd hate anything to happen to you,' she said fondly.

Comet nuzzled her arm and she breathed in his sweet apple scented breath.

'Hey! What do you think you're doing, letting your dog scare my herd like that!' called an angry voice.

Eleanor looked up to see a girl coming towards them on a bay pony with a white star on its forehead. She looked about twelve years old and was frowning fiercely. Luckily, she seemed to have missed Comet's magic display.

'It wasn't my . . .' Eleanor began.

But the girl was too angry to listen. 'Not your fault, eh? Don't you know the forest code? All dogs have to be kept on leads!'

'I know. I've seen the signs. I was trying to tell you that it wasn't my dog!' Eleanor said patiently. She mounted Comet so she could explain to the girl properly from up on her horse. 'It just came out of nowhere. I don't know who it belongs to, but Comet scared it off because the ponies were about to bolt.'

56

'Oh, I didn't realize.' The girl's face
cleared and she looked embarrassed. 'It
was good of you to get him to do that.
Sorry, I tend to speak first and think later.'

'That's OK. It was an easy mistake,'
Eleanor said generously.

'Nice of you to say so. You could easily
have chewed my head off about it!'

'I'm not that hungry!' Eleanor joked.

They both laughed.

The girl introduced herself. 'I'm
Francine Boyd but everyone calls me
Frankie. That's a gorgeous pony you've
got there. Is he forest-bred?'

'Um . . . yeah. Comet's pretty special,'
Eleanor said, smiling to herself. *If only
Frankie knew how much!* 'I'm Eleanor Gale.
I'm staying at Oak Cottage with my Aunt
Pippa for the school holidays,' she said,

changing the subject quickly and hoping
to avoid any more awkward questions.

Frankie nodded. 'I thought I hadn't
seen you round here before. Your aunt's
a photographer, isn't she? Dad said that a
woman who takes brilliant photos of the
forest ponies had moved into the empty
cottage.'

'That's right. Aunt Pippa's got an

exhibition in town next week,' Eleanor
said, smiling at Frankie.

Now the misunderstanding had been
cleared up, the older girl seemed really
friendly. Eleanor hoped Frankie might be
someone she could get to know better.
It was brilliant having Comet as a friend,
but it would be extra fun to have a pony-
mad friend!

Frankie returned her smile. 'I was just
going to have my lunch. Would you like
to share it with me?' she offered. 'It's such
a lovely day that I brought a picnic with
me. I often do when I'm out on Jake,
checking on our ponies. There's a pretty
stream near here. The ponies can have a
drink while we sit and eat.'

'Sounds great, thanks,' Eleanor said
delightedly. 'Is that OK with you?' she

whispered to Comet so that Frankie couldn't hear.

Comet nickered an agreement. 'I would like to stop for a while.'

As Frankie moved forward on Jake, Comet pricked his ears and followed. Eleanor reached forward to pat his silky neck.

'I'm glad we met Frankie,' she whispered.

'Me too. I like her,' Comet neighed enthusiastically.

Eleanor looked up in alarm to see if Frankie had heard him speak.

Comet seemed to know what she was thinking. 'Do not worry, Eleanor. Only you can hear what I am saying. To anyone else it sounds like a neigh or a snort.'

'Oh, that's all right then,' Eleanor

whispered back, hiding a grin.

Comet was full of surprises. She wondered what else he could do.

Sunlight slanted through the trees and made dancing yellow coins of light on the grass path as Eleanor, Comet, Frankie and Jake rode along together. Eleanor felt a stir of happiness. There was nothing better in the whole world than to be out riding on such a glorious morning – especially on a magic pony!

Chapter
FIVE

Eleanor felt nicely full as she lay on her stomach in the warm grass. Frankie's cheese and tomato sandwiches and chocolate brownies washed down with apple juice had been delicious.

It was beautiful in the grove under the spreading beech trees, with the stream bubbling over rocks some distance away. After a long drink of cool water, Comet

was nibbling a patch of sweet grass a few
metres away. Frankie's pony, Jake, stood
beneath a tree, dozing in the shade.

Eleanor had just finished telling
Frankie about her aunt's three ponies.
'They're called Mary, Jed and Blue. We're
going out looking for them after lunch. I
hope we get to see them.'

Frankie laughed. 'Well, don't hold your
breath! Forest ponies can wander off and

be gone for weeks and then just when you think you'll never see them again, they'll start hanging about at the end of your road for ages. It's a good thing your aunt's got Comet too so you can ride him while you're staying with her. I'd hate it if I couldn't ride.'

'Me too. It's what I love doing the most,' Eleanor said. She thought it best to let Frankie assume that Comet belonged to Aunt Pippa, otherwise she didn't know how she was going to explain him. 'How many ponies do you own?'

'We've got fifty at the moment. I won't tell you all their names, you'll never remember them!' Frankie said, grinning.

'Fifty!' Eleanor echoed. 'How do you keep track of them all?'

'It takes practice, but I'm used to

it. We've always had forest ponies.
Our family have been commoners
for generations. Dad's great-great-
grandmother had six mares. All our
ponies are descended from those.'

'Wow! That must have been a *really*
long time ago.' Eleanor was deeply
impressed. She'd love to live in the forest
and work among the ponies like Frankie
and her family. It would be her dream job
when she grew up.

Eleanor glanced at her watch.

'Oh heck! Look at the time. I've been
gone ages. Aunt Pippa will be wondering
where I am. I'd better go!'

'You can blame me for making you
late by inviting you to lunch, if you
like!' Frankie said cheerfully. 'It's the
least I could do after blaming you for

that loose dog. Why don't I ride back
to Oak Cottage with you? I can explain
everything to your aunt.'

Eleanor was tempted. She was eager
to spend more time with this friendly
girl and her pony, but she could hardly
ride up to her aunt's house on Comet.
She imagined trying to explain to her
astonished aunt how she came to be
riding a fully tacked-up pony.

'Thanks, but I'll be fine,' Eleanor said,
hoping that with luck she and Comet
might even beat Aunt Pippa back to the
cottage.

'OK then, but if your aunt gets into a
mega-stress with you, get her to phone
me!' Frankie gave Eleanor her number.
'Are you busy tomorrow? I could call for
you tomorrow morning and show you

around the forest, if you like. I know all
the best rides.'

'I'd love that,' Eleanor said, mounting
Comet. 'Bye for now!' she called, as he
broke into a trot.

'Bye!' Frankie called after them.

Comet had no trouble finding his way
back. He stopped in a clump of trees just
out of sight of the cottage to let Eleanor
dismount. The moment her feet touched
the ground, the tack disappeared in a
small shower of sparks.

'It's a shame you can't make yourself
invisible or something, then you wouldn't
have to hide in the forest. You could stay
here in the back garden and I'd be able
to sneak out and see you all the time,'
Eleanor suggested.

Comet blinked his intelligent violet

eyes. 'That is an interesting idea. I will try out these new powers. I am not yet sure about all the things I can do in this world,' he mused.

Eleanor felt a surge of affection for the chestnut pony. She reached up and gave him a swift hug. 'Maybe we'll find out more about your magical powers together?'

Comet twitched his ears. 'Yes, Eleanor. I think we will.'

Eleanor lowered her arms and stood back. 'I'd better go. I'll come out to you again soon and we can look for Destiny again,' she promised.

'Very well.' Comet tossed his mane and sped away.

Eleanor watched him until he was out of sight and then walked out into the open. She was opening the garden gate when her aunt came out of the kitchen.

'Oh, there you are, Eleanor. I hope you haven't been too bored,' Pippa said.

Eleanor smiled. 'I've been fine. I had a great time . . . um, exploring.' If her aunt only knew!

Pippa suddenly looked at her in astonishment. 'Why on earth are you wearing your riding kit?'

Eleanor could have kicked herself.
She'd completely forgotten about the
boots and hat! She thought quickly.
'I was . . . erm, in the garden when
Frankie Boyd came past on Jake,' she
said, improvising madly. 'We got chatting
about her family's ponies and stuff and
she offered to let me ride one of them.
So I ran inside to get my kit, while she
went to fetch it. We didn't go far, just for
a short hack.'

Her aunt smiled. 'I'm glad you met
Frankie – you were safe enough in the
forest with her. The Boyds are well
respected round here. It sounds like you
had a good time. I'm glad the two of
you got on well. Especially as I ended up
taking longer than I'd meant to.' Pippa

shook her head slowly. 'I'm starting
to think that I should postpone this
exhibition until after you've gone home.
It's not fair on you to have to spend so
much time by yourself.'

'I don't mind!' Eleanor said quickly,
sensing an opportunity. 'Besides, I don't
have to, now that I've met Frankie. She's
calling for me tomorrow.'

'It sounds like you and Frankie have got
things all worked out,' Pippa said, smiling.

'We have!' Eleanor replied spiritedly.

Pippa put her arm round Eleanor's
shoulders and they went into the cottage
together. 'To be honest, I'm relieved. I was
starting to worry that you'd get bored and
wish you hadn't come to stay after all.'

'I wouldn't think that, Aunt Pippa. I
love being here with you!' Eleanor

assured her truthfully. She didn't mind at all that her aunt was so busy. It meant she could spend lots of time with her new magical friend.

'I'm very glad about that,' Pippa said, smiling fondly. She handed Eleanor a paper bag, which Eleanor hadn't noticed until now. 'I was passing a bookshop and I thought you might like this.'

Eleanor opened the bag and took out a book. '*Bumper Book of Horses and Ponies of the World*,' she read. 'Thanks so much. It's brilliant!'

'Time for lunch, I think,' Pippa announced. 'And didn't I promise that we could go out and look for Mary, Jed and Blue this afternoon?'

Eleanor beamed at her aunt, wondering how she was going to eat a second lunch. 'I can't wait!'

Chapter
SIX

Eleanor spent a happy afternoon roaming in the forest with her aunt. They seemed to walk for miles. They often saw glimpses of ponies through the trees and Pippa took a few photographs. Predictably, there was no sign of Jed, Blue or Mary.

That evening, Aunt Pippa cooked a special supper. Eleanor was allowed to help make an apple pie, which made her feel very grown up.

She slipped out into the garden to speak to Comet before she went to bed, but he didn't answer her call. Eleanor guessed he was deep in the forest looking for Destiny and couldn't hear her.

That night she had a vivid dream. In it she saw Destiny disguised as a forest pony, galloping along one of the winding trails, Comet's twin sister leapt across a stream and left a single glowing violet hoof-print in the soft mud. Eleanor awoke abruptly, with the strangest feeling that her dream was true. She decided she would tell Comet tomorrow morning.

The next day Eleanor got up early. After breakfast she said goodbye to her aunt. 'I'm off to meet Frankie. See you later!'

'Have a good time!' Pippa called,
waving.

Eleanor walked a little way into the
forest and called to Comet. She planned
to ride him out of sight of the cottage
to meet up with Frankie where they'd
parted yesterday.

Comet stepped out of the trees and
snorted and tossed his mane.

'Hello, Comet!' she greeted him
warmly. She noticed some small patches
of dried mud on his side. Picking a large
handful of sweet dried grass, she began
brushing him down. 'I came out to see
you last night before I went to bed,
but you'd gone. Were you looking for
Destiny?'

Comet nodded. 'I searched for a long
time.'

'Did you find any signs of her?' Eleanor
asked him.

Comet shook his head sadly. 'I saw
many more ponies, but Destiny was
not with them. And I did not find any
glowing hoof-prints to show that she had
passed by.'

'But I think I did!' Eleanor said
excitedly. 'I saw Destiny in a dream. She

left a glowing hoof-print in the mud near a stream. It's almost like Destiny sent me a message in my sleep!'

Comet's bright violet eyes lit up with fresh hope as he reached round to nuzzle Eleanor's arm. 'Perhaps she did. It would be just like her!'

Eleanor smiled, pleased to see that he looked less despondent. 'We can keep a lookout for her today while we're out with Frankie and Jake.' She twitched the last traces of mud away and then threw the grass down. 'There, finished.'

'Thank you, Eleanor.'

She felt a familiar tingling down her spine as deep violet sparkles glimmered once again in Comet's chestnut coat. When they faded, he was fully tacked up, like last time. Eleanor mounted and they set off at a canter.

They were just in time. Frankie and
Jake were riding towards them through
the trees.

'Hi!' The girls greeted each other, while
Comet and Jake touched noses – saying
hello in pony fashion.

'It looks like Comet and Jake are
already friends!' Frankie said, grinning as
they set off, riding abreast.

It was fun to ride into the heart of the forest with Frankie and weave through narrow, lesser-known trails without worrying about getting lost. They glimpsed a number of wild ponies, spread out among the trees. 'That herd belongs to one of our neighbours, Mr Toms,' Frankie commented.

'How do you know?' Eleanor asked. She was glad of a reason to stop, so that Comet could check if Destiny was one of them.

Frankie explained that you could recognize different commoners' ponies by the way their tails were cut. 'See that one?' She pointed to a grey pony that stood with its back to them. Its tail was cut into a series of blunt steps. 'All of the Tomses' ponies have their tails trimmed like that.'

Comet had been looking round.
'Destiny is not here.' He blew air out of
his nostrils sadly.

Eleanor patted his neck as he rode
down a track, which was bordered by
hedges of hawthorn and brambles and
then opened out in a long, flat clearing. It
was a clear run that stretched to the edge
of some open fields.

'We can let the ponies have their heads
here,' Frankie said, urging Jake on.

'Yay!' Eleanor yelled, pressing Comet
into a gallop.

She could sense the magic pony's
enjoyment as he went flat out. He was
exciting to ride and she loved the feeling
of the wind whistling past them.

'That was brilliant!' she said when they

had slowed their ponies to a trot.

Frankie smiled. 'Wait until you see where we're going next!' She led the way to where there were some fallen logs. 'I often come here to practise jumping,' she said. 'Jake loves it. Watch this.'

She pressed her pony on so that Jake sped up and easily cleared the log. Frankie patted the bay pony's neck. 'Good boy! Now you!' she urged Eleanor. 'Let's see what Comet can do!'

Eleanor clicked her tongue. Comet didn't hesitate. He leapt forward. Three strides, two strides, one stride . . .

Comet soared through the air and landed safely on the other side of the log.

'Way to go! He almost looked like was flying!' Frankie exclaimed.

Eleanor bit back a grin.

'You were fantastic!' she whispered to
him with her back to Frankie.

'I enjoyed it too,' Comet said.

The ponies took it in turns to go over
the jumps. After a stop for lunch and a

chance for the ponies to have a drink,
they went for a more leisurely ride along
the grass verge beside one of the public
roads.

As the afternoon wore on, the girls
and ponies headed back to Oak Cottage.
Eleanor halted under cover of the trees to
say goodbye to Frankie and Jake. 'Thanks
so much. We had a brilliant time! Shall we
meet up again tomorrow?'

'I don't think I can. Some of the
commoners are having a round-up,'
Frankie explained. 'It can get a bit hectic
so I'll probably have to give Dad a hand.
I know! Why don't you and Comet come
and watch? It's pretty exciting. Visitors
aren't usually allowed, but you'll be OK
with me. I'll square it with Dad. It'll be
great for you to see so many forest ponies

in one place.'

'I wouldn't miss it for anything!'

Eleanor waved as Frankie rode away.

Chapter
SEVEN

That evening it pelted with rain – a dense downpour that lasted for hours and cast a dark veil over the forest.

Eleanor was curled up on the squishy sofa, reading her new horse and pony book, but she couldn't concentrate for worrying about Comet. She knew he'd probably be sheltering under the trees, like the other sturdy forest ponies, but

unlike them he was all alone and missing
Destiny.

Her aunt was working in her office at
the front of the house, so Eleanor decided
to risk going outside to check on Comet.
Grabbing an umbrella, she hurried
through the back garden and entered the
forest clearing.

'Comet,' she called softly.

There was no answer. No chestnut
pony stepped out of the trees and came
towards her. She waited a little longer, but
the magic pony still didn't appear.

'Comet? Where are you?' Eleanor
called again and then she thought she
heard his voice, but it was very faint as if
it came from far away.

'I am here . . .'

Where was he? Puzzled, Eleanor went

back into the house. She decided that
she would have to wait until morning
to go out and look for him. She was just
dumping the dripping umbrella into
the stand in the hall when she heard his
gentle whinny again.

'Eleanor. Come closer. I am here . . .'

Comet sounded a tiny bit louder than
before and he seemed to be calling from
upstairs. Curiously, Eleanor went up to
her bedroom.

She stood in the open doorway and
looked around. She could sense that
something was different, but what? Her
gaze fell on the table next to her bed.
There beneath the lamp stood a little toy
horse with a fluffy chestnut coat, a pale
mane and tail, and sparkling deep violet
eyes.

As Eleanor watched, the toy horse
shook itself and twitched its tail.

'Comet?' Eleanor gasped. 'Is it really
you? That's so cool!'

'I found another way of using my
magic!' Comet told her proudly in a tiny
soft neigh that matched his new size.
She smiled delightedly at her amazing
friend. 'Now you can stay in my room

whenever you like and sleep on my bed.
I can even carry you in my shoulder bag
and take you out with me!'

'I did not think of that. It sounds like it
would be fun!' Comet said.

Eleanor picked him up very gently
and sat on the patchwork quilt with him
on her lap. Comet was handsome as a
chestnut pony and very beautiful as his
true golden-winged self – but right now
he was the cutest and fluffiest miniature
pony she had ever seen.

She was so engrossed in admiring
Comet's tiny neat hooves and little
pointed ears that she didn't notice the
bedroom door swing open.

'I thought I heard you come up here.
I was just going to make some hot
chocolate and wondered if . . . Goodness

me! What *have* you got there?' Aunt Pippa
exclaimed, her eyes widening.

Eleanor froze in shock, but it was too
late to hide Comet.

'It's . . . um . . . I was just . . .' she
faltered. Her mind was a total blank.

'What a gorgeous little toy pony!'
Pippa's face softened as she came forward.
'It's perfect in every detail. Did Frankie
give it to you?' she asked.

Aunt Pippa thinks Comet is a toy? Huh?
Eleanor frowned in confusion. She could
feel Comet's heartbeat against her fingers
and see him twitching his ears and tail.
She couldn't believe that her aunt hadn't
noticed.

'Um . . . yeah. It's cute, isn't it? I've
called him Comet,' she said. 'It was nice
of Frankie – I really like her. She's asked

me to go out again with her tomorrow.
There's going to be a round-up of some
of the commoners' ponies. She said that I
could go and watch.'

'You really are pony-mad, aren't you?'
Pippa said, looking thoughtful.

'Yep! Ponies are the most wonderful
things in the entire universe!' Eleanor
sang out.

Her aunt laughed fondly. 'I won't argue with that!'

Eleanor quickly slipped Comet behind her back and gently tucked him between her pillows, just in case her aunt felt like looking at him more closely.

'You'll enjoy the round-up,' Pippa said. 'The Boyd herd has the best pedigree around here. Their ponies fetch good prices. There'll be other commoners with their herds there too. I think I'll come with you. It'll be a chance to get some good photographs.'

'Sounds good,' Eleanor said, so relieved by the change of subject that she wasn't really concentrating. As soon as her aunt had gone downstairs to make the hot chocolate, she turned to Comet. 'Phew! I nearly had kittens when she came in.

What just happened? I don't get it.'

'I used my magic again, so that only you can see me move and hear me speak,' Comet said. 'Anyone else will think that I am just a fluffy toy.'

'I never know what to expect with you. I love having you as a friend,' Eleanor said, grinning from ear to ear. Suddenly, her face fell. 'Oh heck. Did Aunt Pippa just say that she was coming with us tomorrow to take photos of the ponies during the round-up?'

Comet nodded his tiny head. 'I think that she did.'

Eleanor groaned. 'Oh no!'

So far she had managed to keep Aunt Pippa away from Frankie so that her aunt wouldn't find out about Comet being a life-size pony! She chewed her lip as she wondered what might happen when the older girl and her aunt got talking, as they were bound to do tomorrow.

What on earth was she going to do?

Chapter
EIGHT

'There's nothing for it. I'm going to have to walk over to meet Frankie and think of some excuse as to why I'm not riding you,' Eleanor decided as she fastened her boots the following day. 'I just hope that Frankie doesn't start asking Aunt Pippa where *her* pony Comet is. And why I'm not riding him today!'

'Thank you for helping me, Eleanor. I

know it has not always been easy for you,'
Comet said gratefully.

'I wouldn't have it any other way,'
Eleanor said fondly, stroking the tiny
pony's fluffy coat. 'It's a shame you have
to stay behind, though. There's a good
chance that with so many ponies about,
you'd find Destiny among them.'

'I think so too. That is why I *am* going
to come with you,' Comet said.

'But how? You can't do that without
giving yourself away —' Eleanor stopped
as she realized what Comet meant — 'Oh,
I get it. You're going to use your magic to
stay as a fluffy toy? Great idea. I'll get my
shoulder bag!'

She found the bag and laid it on the
floor with the top open. Comet jumped
inside, lay down and folded his legs

beneath him.

Downstairs, Aunt Pippa was ready to go. She was holding her camera. 'All set?' she said, smiling as Eleanor came in with her bag over her shoulder.

Eleanor nodded.

Pippa smiled warmly. 'We'll soon be able to have lots more days out. My exhibition's almost up and running now. I really appreciate how you've been so

patient and understanding about having
to entertain yourself.'

'That's OK. I was never bored,' Eleanor
said. There was no chance of that with
Comet around!

The forest smelt fresh and new. Large
drops were dripping from the trees after
last night's heavy rain. But the sunshine
was already drying the ground underfoot
as Eleanor, Comet and Pippa set out to
walk towards the round-up area.

'We'll go this way. It's a short-cut,' Aunt
Pippa said, turning on to a stony track
that wound between tall field maples.

They had been walking for about ten
minutes when Pippa suddenly stopped.

'Well, look at that,' she whispered,
pointing to three ponies that were
cropping the short grass. 'There's Jed, Blue

and Mary. They always turn up when you least expect it.'

Eleanor watched delightedly as her aunt called to her wild ponies. Recognizing her voice, they lifted their heads, ears twitching. As they walked towards Pippa, Eleanor saw they were all wearing their fluorescent collars for night safety.

'It's best if you keep your distance. They know me, but it can be dangerous for a stranger to approach them,' Pippa warned.

'They're gorgeous,' Eleanor said, admiring her aunt's ponies. Mary was a dark bay with a gentle face; Jed was a lively-looking grey with a black tail, and Blue was a sweet little brown pony with black points.

Pippa took some slices of apple and

carrot out of her pocket. 'I always have
some treats with me,' she told Eleanor.
Her ponies munched happily for a few
moments, then, as Pippa, Eleanor and
Comet walked on, they went back to
grazing.

'I'm glad I got to see them at last,'
Eleanor said.

She and her aunt continued down

the path, which widened and opened
into an oval-shaped clearing ringed with
flowering bushes. Eleanor opened her
shoulder bag, so that Comet could look
out as they walked.

Aunt Pippa noticed Comet's tiny
legs, which were looped over the bag's
opening, and smiled. 'How sweet. You've
brought Comet with you!' she observed.

Eleanor nodded, smiling. 'You're . . . er,
never too old for a cuddly toy.'

The sounds of voices and ponies came
towards them through the trees, and
Eleanor knew they must be getting close
to the round-up area.

Suddenly, she did a double-take and
stopped dead.

Stretching ahead of them and curving
out of sight was a faint line of softly

glowing violet hoof-prints.

Eleanor heard Comet's excited voice from inside her bag. 'Destiny! She has been here!'

Eleanor gasped. Did that mean that Comet was leaving to go after her? 'Can you tell where she is? Is she somewhere close?' she whispered to him anxiously.

'No. The trail is cold. But it proves that Destiny came this way. When I am close to where she is, I will be able to hear her hoof-beats. And I may have to leave suddenly . . . without saying goodbye.'

'Oh.' Eleanor felt a sharp pang as she realized that she would never be ready to lose her magical friend. 'I was hoping that once you had found Destiny, you might both stay here with me,' she said in a small voice.

Comet shook his head. 'It is not possible. We have to return to our family on Rainbow Mist Island. I hope you understand, Eleanor?'

Eleanor nodded sadly and her eyes pricked with tears. She swallowed hard as she decided not to think about Comet leaving and promised herself instead that she was going to enjoy every single moment spent with him.

Up ahead, Aunt Pippa had stopped to wait for her. 'Is something wrong, love?' she asked, frowning with concern at Eleanor's glum face.

'No, I'm . . . er, fine,' Eleanor said, making a big effort to cheer up. 'I had a stitch in my side, but it's gone now.'

'Good. We're almost there now.'

Eleanor hurried to catch up with her aunt. The sounds of voices, ponies snorting and car doors slamming were even louder. Despite herself, Eleanor found herself looking forward to seeing Frankie and Jake again.

They emerged to one side of a group of buildings and wooden pens, some of them already filled with ponies of all ages.

Cars and trucks were parked all around
and lots of people stood around in groups.
Others were watching their ponies being
treated by vets.

'Hi, Eleanor!'

It was Frankie. She was standing next
to a large pen with a man who looked
so much like her that he had to be her
father.

Eleanor waved, grinning, and she and
her aunt began walking towards them.

Just then two men on horseback
appeared. They were trying to get a herd
of nervous ponies to go into an empty
pen. There was a sudden loud bang as a
car backfired. A large roan pony rolled
its eyes and squealed in fright. It plunged
sideways, avoiding the pen. Other ponies
followed it, blindly galloping after the big

roan in their terror.

The horsemen wheeled, trying to get control. But it was too late. People scattered in all directions as the ponies stampeded.

'Look out!' someone shouted.

Eleanor gasped. The ponies were thundering straight towards her and Aunt Pippa. And Comet couldn't use his magic to save them without giving himself away!

Chapter
NINE

'Quick! Eleanor! Get behind a tree!' Aunt
Pippa shouted to Eleanor.

With only seconds to spare, Eleanor
leapt sideways, but her foot skidded on
a wet leaf and she went sprawling. Her
shoulder bag slipped off and the toy pony
fell out and rolled over and over, coming
to rest under a bush.

As Eleanor struggled to her feet, she

felt the now familiar tingling sensation
fizz in the tips of her fingers and saw the
bush sparkle with pretty violet light.

Time seemed to stand still.

Comet exploded out of the trees. He
leapt towards Eleanor, shielding her

with his body as he faced the oncoming ponies. Rearing up on to his hind legs, he whinnied a warning.

The ponies swerved in all directions, pounding past Eleanor and narrowly missing her with their flying hooves. The second they were past, Comet glanced at Eleanor to check that she was unhurt and streaked away into the forest.

Aunt Pippa ran over and helped Eleanor to stand up as men on horseback galloped past them in pursuit of the loose ponies.

'Are you hurt?' her aunt asked, white-faced.

'No. I'm fine. Just a bit shaken up,' Eleanor said, catching her breath. *Thanks to Comet*, she thought.

'That chestnut pony came out of

nowhere, but I'm very glad it did! It saved you from a nasty injury. I wonder who it belongs to,' Aunt Pippa said.

Eleanor didn't answer.

Just then, Frankie ran up too. 'Eleanor! What happened? We couldn't see back there.'

'The loose ponies missed me. I'm OK now. The show's over!' Eleanor joked, to show that she really was fine. Hoping that everyone would stop fussing, she walked determinedly towards the pony pens. 'Come on. I don't want to miss anything!' she called.

They reached the pens just as a man holding a clipboard made an announcement. The pony sale was about to begin. An air of excitement hung over the crowd as the bids started.

Frankie's dad came over to introduce himself. 'You must be Eleanor. Frankie's told me about you.'

Eleanor smiled at him. 'Hi. Pleased to meet you, Mr Boyd.'

Mr Boyd turned to Aunt Pippa. 'I'm a great admirer of your photographs, Ms Treacy. I look forward to seeing your exhibition.'

'Thanks. Nice of you to say so,' Pippa said, smiling. 'I'm hoping to take a few photographs today . . . among other things,' she said mysteriously, looking sideways at Eleanor.

Eleanor frowned, puzzled. What did her aunt have in mind?

But before she could find out, Eleanor heard a sound she had been hoping for and dreading at the same time.

The hollow sound of galloping hooves overhead.

She froze. Destiny! There was no mistake. And if Eleanor could hear her, then Comet must be very close.

Eleanor set off into the forest at a run. 'There's something I have to do!' she called over her shoulder.

She raced through the trees. The magical hoof-beats sounded louder and very close now.

As she reached a thick clump of bushes, a twinkling rainbow mist floated down around her. She looked up to see Comet in his true form – a sturdy chestnut pony no longer. Sunlight gleamed on his noble head, magnificent golden wings and cream coat. His flowing mane and tail sparkled like strands of spun silk.

'Comet!' Eleanor gasped. She had almost forgotten how beautiful he was as a Lightning Horse. 'You're leaving right now, aren't you?' she asked, her voice breaking.

Comet's deep violet eyes lost a little of their twinkle as he smiled sadly. 'I must, if

I am to catch Destiny and save her from our enemies.'

A heavy wave of sadness washed over Eleanor as she knew she was going to have to be brave. She ran forward and threw her arms round Comet's shining neck. 'I'll never forget you!'

He allowed her to hug him one last time and then gently stepped backwards. 'Farewell, my young friend. Ride well and true,' he said in a deep musical voice.

There was a final violet flash of light and a silent fountain of rainbow sparkles fell like soft rain around Eleanor, crackling as they hit the ground. Comet spread his wings and soared upwards. He faded and was gone.

Eleanor wiped her eyes. Something glittered on the ground. It was a single shimmering wing-feather. Reaching down, she picked it up.

It tingled against her palm as it faded to a cream colour. Eleanor tucked the feather into her pocket. She would always keep it to remind herself of the wonderful adventure she and Comet had shared. She was so proud that the magic pony had chosen to be her friend.

When Eleanor stepped out of the trees, Frankie ran up to her. 'There you are. Your aunt's looking for you!'

Eleanor looked over Frankie's shoulder to where her aunt stood holding a gorgeous chestnut pony by its head collar. The pony had a sandy mane and tail and gentle deep brown eyes. 'Come and meet my new pony, Eleanor. It's time I bought one to ride, and you can exercise

her whenever you come and stay with
me. I think perhaps you deserve a pony in
your life aside from Comet.'

'Wow!' whistled Frankie. 'How lucky
are you?'

Eleanor grinned as she realized Frankie
didn't know that her aunt was referring

to what she thought was her niece's toy
pony.

'How would you like to choose her
name?'

Eleanor thought of Comet on his
journey to find his twin sister. She hoped
they were reunited soon. 'Thank you
so much, Aunt Pippa. I'd like to call her
Destiny.'

Coming Soon

Magic Ponies

A Twinkle
of Hooves

Showjumping
Dreams

puffin.co.uk

Win a Magic Ponies goody bag!

Golden feathers from Comet's wings are falling out as he desperately tries to find his twin sister, Destiny, who is still lost in our world! The feathers carry a secret message for Destiny.

Two words from the message can be found in magic golden feathers hidden in *A New Friend* and *A Special Wish*.

To help save Destiny from danger, find the hidden words and put them together to complete the message. Send it in to us and each month we will put every correct message in a draw and pick out one lucky winner to receive a whole stable of Magic Ponies goodies!

Send your secret message, name and address on a postcard to:

Magic Ponies competition

Puffin Books

80 Strand

London WC2R 0RL

Please help Comet save his sister!

Good luck!

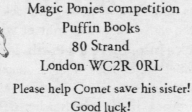

puffin.co.uk

It all started with a Scarecrow

Puffin is well over sixty years old.
Sounds ancient, doesn't it? But Puffin has never been
so lively. We're always on the lookout for the next big
idea, which is how it began all those years ago.

Penguin Books was a big idea from the mind of
a man called Allen Lane, who in 1935 invented
the quality paperback and changed the world.
**And from great Penguins, great Puffins grew,
changing the face of children's books forever.**

The first four Puffin Picture Books were hatched in 1940 and the
first Puffin story book featured a man with broomstick arms called
Worzel Gummidge. In 1967 Kaye Webb, Puffin Editor, started the
Puffin Club, promising to **'make children into readers'.**
She kept that promise and over 200,000 children became
devoted Puffineers through their quarterly installments of
Puffin Post, which is now back for a new generation.

Many years from now, we hope you'll look back and
remember Puffin with a smile. **No matter what your age
or what you're into, there's a Puffin for everyone.**
The possibilities are endless, but one thing is for sure:
whether it's a picture book or a paperback, a sticker book
or a hardback, **if it's got that little Puffin
on it – it's bound to be good.**